MaGPie

Bridge
I Am ~~Just~~ Not Junco
BOOK FIVE

By J. A. Huss

MaGPie

Bridge
I Am ~~Just~~ Not Junco
BOOK FIVE
By J. A. Huss
Find me at
New Adult Addiction

Edited by RJ Locksley
Cover design by J. A. Huss and James Ledger

ISBN-13: 978-1-944475-75-8

Dedication

To all the nerdy, geeky people who love this SF shit, birds, and dark books with a touch a realism, hot winged dudes, and psycho girls named Junco as much as I do. Because I love the fuck out of SF, birds, dark, gritty books, hot winged dudes, and psycho girls named Junco.

Chapter One

The high-altitude wind whips past my face, leaving it raw and dry as I watch the scene play out down below. I cross my arms in front of my chest and ask my pupils to dilate and then contract, trying to keep Junco in focus as she makes the walk to the waiting pillar of light.

"What's she doing?"

I look over and see Arel and Annun, looking at me and down at the valley, respectively. I sigh in the general direction of my brother, although my eyes never find his face, and shrug. "I'm not sure, Arel."

"Was this part of the plan?"

"Not our plan."

"Gideon?"

Sometimes Arel can really piss me off with his questions. It's like he's got no internal filter. Just spews out words without thinking. "Do I look like I know Gideon's plan?" I hiss at him.

He ignores my mood, as per usual, and just lets out a long whistle. "This is about to get interesting."

It's hard to upset Arel. Even with the existence of our entire race on the line, he can shrug it off. "Interesting?" I scoff. "That's one way to put it."

Annun spits on the ground and comes around to the other side of me. "You think she knows what she's doing?"

I want to rip his fucking head off and my hands are even reaching for his throat when I stop. Annun just spits again and pretends it never happened. I think he's been spending too much time with Arel.

"I mean," he continues, "she's typically got a handle on stuff, right? Even when you think she's fucked and lost her mind, she pulls through, right?"

He's right. On most days Junco pulls through. She's tough. She's powerful. She's a force.

"She's Junco, for fuck's sake," Annun continues, more to himself than any of us.

But today is not most days. Today was *her* day. The day she's been waiting for.

Lucan appears by my side and we let out a collective sigh as her body begins to glow, then Inanna's follows suit. Seconds later they are gone.

"Well, that's pretty much it, then." Arel flips open his tablet and begins punching in data.

I wait, not looking at, nor acknowledging, Lucan. Because if I want to be truthful, Lucan's the one I want to rip apart, not Annun. I want to blame him. Just fucking once, I want to make it all his fault, tell him off, push back and walk away. Just once I want to lose control instead of standing by his side.

"Ten meters per second and slowing." Arel slaps the tablet shut, like that's the end of it. "This one is not on track for completion, initiation is delayed by one point five minutes for every minute completion fails." He looks up to me and shrugs. "We're stuck until she finishes whatever she's doing in there. I'm assuming she's slicing her mother to bits? But maybe not. They could be having a fucking picnic for all I know."

He disappears, leaving Annun behind.

Annun barely notices, just spits one more time and picks up where he left off. "Take the Deliverance fight for instance. She went into that with no clue. None. So, I think this time, they maybe have a plan." He looks over to Lucan. "What do ya think, Luc?"

Lucan growls at the nickname and I don't blame him. Annun pushes buttons on purpose, not like Arel who's just being good-natured. Annun is a mean motherfucker and to be honest, he's very lucky I'm tired of constantly kicking his ass, or I really would throttle his throat right now. "Get to fucking work or I'll send ya back to Amelia to babysit."

"He can come with me," Lucan states matter-of-factly. "I'm going back soon to wait it out with her, anyway. She's unhappy. And afraid."

Annun shrugs. "I'll go, sure. Why not."

"Annun," I growl, "your ass is supposed to be scouring the Stag for that child."

"Tier, I like to delegate, right? I have a team down there—"

"What fucking team?"

"Merkar, Pike and Tessen. And I gave each of them a legion of their own. If the kid's down there, we'll find her."

The heat from my eyes tells me they are red. I direct the glow towards Annun.

He disappears.

Lucan turns to me then, but I don't look at him. I've had enough and he knows it. "What's that look?" he asks. "Sadness?"

"Don't, Lucan. I'm at the end here. I asked you for one thing and that was to keep her safe and you go and tell her to *do it her way*." I stop to look him in the eye. "This is her way, Lucan. Congratulations, she did exactly what you told her to do."

"You have very little faith in her, Raubtier. I find it quite disturbing. She always has so much faith in herself, it's a shame you can't see what she's capable of. Besides, Sera is with her, correct? You said she mentioned that."

"Have you talked to Sera?" His expression is unreadable.

"No, not in several weeks, actually. But Junco said—"

"Junco is fucking *sick*, Lucan. Sick." I wait to see if he's got anything to say to that, but if he does, he holds it in.

The cold air is heavy with the silence, and once again I notice that the wind is making my face chapped and raw.

"She's sick. She told me she's got a condition. Some mental disorder that makes her want to count things, or tap things. Some condition that makes her want to count stars and never stop. A compulsion to embrace insanity. Does this make any sense to you?"

A loud boom shakes the mountains and an explosion of light erupts from the top of the Pillar. The ground shakes and snow begins to slide down a nearby mountain where it's gotten too deep from the early fall snow.

"Fuck!" I look over at Lucan. "What the fuck was that?" I call Arel to come back via vision screen and watch Lucan's surprised face as he studies the sky. It looks like a fireworks display—particles shooting out of the top of the Pillar and up into space.

Arel appears and his fingers are in mid-slide across his tablet. I wait as they fly across the screen and then he looks up at me and shakes his head. "Dissipation particles. That crazy little sparrow fucking dissipated her ass!" He barks out a laugh and looks up at the light show in the sky. "She fucking dissipated Inanna!"

I look up as well, a slight wave of relief washing through my heart when Arel's voice interrupts my almost celebration. "Wait. There's two sets of particles, not one—"

He doesn't finish his sentence. He doesn't have to because this can only mean one thing.

They scattered each other.

I enter the timeshift before my anger can manifest as knives and fangs.

Chapter Two

I've never been to New Peak City and I only went to the old one a few times when I was here watching Juncs. But my body finds the Circus like I've been there every day of my life. I even exit sitting on the side of the fountain, my face in my hands. Lost.

The people around me begin to panic and the screaming starts. I'm not the most popular guy on the planet right now. Something to do with millions dying in the floods I've unleashed with the Pillars. Why they're still here, I have no idea. Technically, if all went well, the Pillar eruption should've been well on its way to demolishing New Peak City in a massive earthquake, just like Subjack blew up the old one with a nuclear bomb.

I raise my head for a moment to take in the bedlam, then let it sink back into my hands.

I knew this moment with Junco was coming. I mean, she was one hundred percent honest about the way she saw her future when we were out on the red rock. She told me exactly how she'd meet her destiny, I just never suspected it would be in the Pillar. I never suspected she'd even consider taking Inanna in there because I counted on her finishing the job. It's not like her really, to leave her job unfinished. And after all those words to Irin about the mission keeping her sane, I figured I had time to change her mind. To tell her I'll be there—that I will *find a way* to be there.

I scrub my face with my hands Tand allow the grief to wash over me. My whole chest hurts. Like hands are crushing me to death. Twisting up my heart and making every breath a struggle. I have no frame of reference for this feeling. It is dread. Overpowering dread, and hopelessness and sadness. I feel like a part of me is gone. And this is nothing like the moment when we all realized Inanna had taken Junco for the morph or even those years she was in the tank. Because I knew where she was and I knew she'd be back. No matter what, I knew that one day *she'd be back.*

But this time I can't count on that.

I've failed her.

Again.

It's not Lucan's fault for handing her his trust. It's my fault for not hearing her last cry for help.

I'd rather float in the nothingness and drift away for eternity than get a stay of execution on my unhappy ending, Tier. I'm tired and I just want it to be over.

How much clearer could she have made it?

I heard what I wanted to hear. A hypothetical. Not the promise she was making.

When the shooting starts I begin to get annoyed, but it takes rapid fire and plasmas to make me give a shit. I put up a shield and don't even bother to watch the feeble attempts of the New Peak City security to kill me, I just continue to hold my head in my hands.

As if it were that fucking easy to kill me now, anyway.

"Why are you here, Beast?"

I force myself to look up and find a small child standing inside my shield perimeter with a pretty severe scowl on her face. She's got shoulder-length brown hair, hazel eyes, a pink shirt, pink flipflops, and some scraggly denim shorts.

"I said—"

"I heard, ya, girl. I'm looking for HOUSE. Junco sent me."

Her whole demeanor changes in an instant. "She did? Where is she? Is she OK? Is she in there?" Her little finger points up to the sky where the light Pillar is still shining up towards the heavens.

I nod. "She's in there. But she wanted me to take ya out of here, so go get your stuff and I'll wait for ya." I look back at the Pillar of light and drop my face in my hands one more time, suddenly exhausted.

And then I feel her fingertips pry one hand off my cheek. "She's dead, isn't she?"

I study her face. The face of Junco at about age eight. I know this because I've seen all her photo albums. I looked at them endlessly over the last two years. At first I'd just sit in her room and look. But eventually I moved all her personal things into my own room to keep them close. I almost moved into her room instead, but she was never there long enough to put any sort of mark on it and besides, Kadian was always spying. "She's not capable of dying, HOUSE. So, no. She's not dead. Now go get your stuff."

She stands there pouting. "I have no stuff."

"No? Well, OK then. Can you leave here? Junco didn't seem to be too sure about that."

"I can leave, I just wanted to take New Peak City for myself. My house was so small in comparison and besides, they made a place for an AI here but she hadn't moved in yet. How could I resist?"

It fucking figures.

It's entirely appropriate that Junco's HOUSE turns out to be a conniving, sneaky little look-a-like who's dead set on getting her way about things. I scoop her up in my arms and we go back into the timeshift together and exit on Gideon's Sargassum terrace.

She squirms in my embrace and I loosen my grip and allow her to slide down. "Wow! Where are we?" She runs to the edge of the terrace, climbs the bottom railing, and leans over. Far over.

My heart thumps a little as I watch her begin to step up on the second railing. "Hey, get the hell off that thing! Put yer feet on the ground, right now!"

She makes no move to obey and I'm crossing the terrace to yank her down when she turns, smiling. "It's far, isn't it? Wow, is this where you live?"

"Very far," I say, grabbing her arm and pulling her off the railing. "And no, this isn't my house, it's Gideon's. I'm looking for him."

She's already run off, squealing her way into the living room yelling something about automated shopping and bathing suits.

It's my turn to lean over the railing. I look down at the black rocks Junco was sitting on when I came here the night of her birthday. I turn my gaze down the beach looking for people, but it's empty. Totally evacuated. They weren't sure what I had planned and since Sargassum is nothing but a floating man-made archipelago, they took the conservative approach and got everyone off the resort before I had a chance to wipe it out with tsunami waves.

I walk back towards the terrace doors and when I reach them, I turn and pace back the other way. I continue this for a while. Just pacing. Thinking. Part of me wants Annun to come back and tell me how Junco's always got a plan. How together she is on the inside. How sneaky she is. That she can pull it off just because she's Junco and she finds a way to pull everything off.

But the rational part sees nothing but the dissipation particles shooting up into the sky like those fountains they have in Vegas.

She's not coming back from this one, Tier. Face it. She's not coming back.

But I've had that thought so often it's becoming cliché. How many times have we sat around and discussed rumors of Junco's demise?

Pretty much once a week since we located her more than four years ago.

She's been dead and gone and then revived and reborn in my mind so many times, I'm not sure what her actual life status is any more.

I look up.

But there's no Halo circling the earth. There's no defense system to protect us. I have no Junco, I have no future that I can see. I have no hope.

There's no hope.

We are fucked.

.

Chapter Three

"Stop! There!" I bark at Ashur. "See that?" My finger points to the scattered particles of dust that are being ejected from the pillar on screen. "That's it, right there."

Ashur squints his eyes a little, a habit I've despised since we were boys. "Tier, man, I sure hope that's not her. I mean, she's done if it is. She's so fucking screwed up, there's no way she'll pull herself back together. It's never gonna happen. And forget the fact that Inanna can't complete the Halo without Junco, *we* can't complete the Halo without Junco. We gotta move on to Plan B already. The ships are beyond capacity, and after three weeks in space people are getting restless."

"No. Not yet."

Lucan appears and leans in. "What are we looking at?"

"Junco," Ashur snorts.

My fist crashes against his face and we go down brawling. "I'm sorry, shit!" he laughs.

Lucan pulls us apart like we're kids again. "Enough."

"Ashur, I swear—"

"Sorry. It's a bad joke, I get it."

"I'm hun-gry!"

Ash and I wince together as we help each other up off the floor.

"Who is *that?*" Lucan asks.

"Junco's HOUSE."

"Hmmm. She does not look like a house, Ashur."

"I'm a girl!" she squeals. That little voice—incessantly asking for things like food, and drinks, and trips to the beach—is really grating on my nerves.

"What are you doing with her, Raubtier?"

"Babysitting for Junco," Ashur answers.

"Would you shut the fuck up? I've had enough of you. I made a promise to get her out of Peaks before the earthquakes."

"What earthquakes?"

"Exactly," Ash answers.

"I'm hun-gry!"

Lucan walks over to her and bends down. "You are *not* hungry, you're an AI. I'm quite versed in AI engineering and maintenance, and they do not require food. So, why don't you keep quiet over here and watch something stupid on the screen so we don't have to listen to your mouth as it flaps up and down and spews things we do not care about?"

Ash smiles at me. "He's got a way with kids, right? Brings back all those awesome memories of being little in Lucan's house."

"Was he an asshole?" the little voice says.

I turn on my heel, fuming and pointing. "I already warned ya once, girl!"

"Junco never cared if I said asshole."

"Say it again," I growl down at her. "I dare ya."

She thinks about this and makes a face just as Lucan walks back over to us. "If there's nothing new here I'll be leaving. When you ditch the child let me know, I'll come back."

And then he's gone.

"Yeah, well, I'm gonna take off, too," Ash says. "I heard Annun say he heard some warrior in South America say someone saw Gideon on a beach in Australia. I'm gonna go check it out later."

"And Sera?"

He shakes out a no. "Nothing on Sera. She's been missing for, shit… since Junco ported out of your room, I think."

"Yeah. I might've been wrong about that, which means I fed Junco some bunk intel and never got to make it right."

He just shrugs. "Ya said she didn't believe you anyway, so fuck it. She's the most powerful thing in this system, Tier, she can handle herself."

I change the subject because that might be true from our perspective, but not from Junco's. She was damaged and desperate when she walked into that Pillar. "Where ya going now?"

"Selia." He says it with some hesitation, like he's trying not to hurt my feelings—his girlfriend is hurt, but recovering. While my—whatever she is—is simply gone.

"She better?"

"Yeah, pretty much. She's not allowed out of medical yet, Layla's orders. But I can visit now and she's walking."

I let out a breath. "That's great, Ash. I'm happy for ya." I ask the obvious, since Caleb was the one who brought her in, mostly healed already. "Has she been… marked?"

He nods. "Yeah, but I don't care, really. It just confirms that she's a good person, ya know? She deserves it. It would be beyond selfish to be angry about something like that."

"Yer a good guy, Ashur. Truly, I'm sorry she got hurt."

"I know. And—" He claps me on the back and then pulls me into a hug. "I take it all back, brother. Junco's diabolical, not crazy. She's got to have a plan, so I'm fine with waiting it out, OK?"

I don't even have a chance to nod before he's gone.

"I'm hun—"

"OK!" I bark, cutting off her annoying whine. "I heard ya the first time, girl. What do ya eat, then?"

"I have a name."

I walk over to her and stand there, towering above her. "HOUSE is not a name, it's a thing. So I'm going to call you girl, because that's a thing too, but at least it describes what ya look like right now."

"It is so a name!" The girl actually stomps a foot in defiance.

"Don't." I poke my finger on her forehead several times as I talk. "I'm in a bad mood. What do ya eat, girl?"

She takes her time to consider this and I'm about to lose any extra patience I might have for Junco's stupid HOUSE when she finally answers. "Peanut butter and jelly. That's what I eat."

"That's disgusting."

She shrugs. "We ate it all the time growing up. Peanut butter was always on the list of allowed foods and—"

That's right. Lucan mentioned that Junco had some weird food rules as a child. No wonder her eating habits are so screwed up.

I look back to the child and HOUSE is still talking. "—oat bread. Is there oat bread in there? Not *wheat* bread," she makes a face, "*oat* bread."

I go to the kitchen and she follows me, her little pink flipflops smacking her heel as she walks. My finger goes down the list on the side of Gideon's excessively stocked autocook and sure enough, there's a number for peanut butter and jelly with oat bread. I enter it into the machine and push start.

"Gideon knows what Junco likes."

I look over the list and I figure she's right. Gideon does know because his menu is mostly filled with crap. Cookies, mac and cheese, some fish, rice, chicken. Like every kind of chicken recipe on Earth. Orange juice, cheeseburgers, French fries, and blueberry pancakes.

I hate Gideon.

The cooker dings and I open it and hand the girl her sandwich, then watch to see if she actually eats it. I think she's pretending to be Junco so that food will sit on the plate and not be touched, but I'm wrong. She scarfs it down like she's starving. I raise my eyebrows at her.

"Told ya," she says, spitting out a small piece of bread as she speaks.

"Don't talk with yer mouth full, didn't Junco teach ya manners?"

"She did," she continues, again with her mouth full. "But you're rude, so you don't count."

"Is that right?"

She only nods this time, her mouth is too full to even spit. I watch her chew for what seems like eternity and then she finally swallows. "Milk," she croaks.

I punch in milk, wait for the beep, and hand it to her.

She guzzles the entire cup and hands it back for a refill.

We stand there like that, her alternating between chewing and drinking. Me watching. Her sending me dirty looks. Me sending her confused ones. Until she's finished and she lets out a big burp.

"Excuse me."

A laugh bursts out unexpectedly and I feel a little bit of the sadness leave for a few moments. I can only imagine what kind of little shit Junco was as a child when I look at this little copy. "You're excused, girl. Go take a nap or something. Don't Earth kids take naps? I want ta look at this footage again."

She yawns. "I am tired."

I point to the bedrooms down the hall. "Find one ya like."

"No, I'll sleep here by you, if that's OK. You might leave without me if I go back there."

"Where would I go?"

She shrugs. "I dunno. But everyone was always leaving Junco behind, and that was never fun. I don't want to be left behind like Junco."

She makes a little crack in my stone heart. "I won't leave, I promise. But you can sleep out here if ya want."

She does want. I settle on the coffee table, my legs stretched out and the touchscreen within easy reach so I can pause the satellite feed frame by frame. HOUSE curls up on the couch, her breath going in and out quickly, and we settle into Evening One of My World Minus Junco— Round Three.

Chapter Four

I watch the footage of dissipation particles above Pillar Seven several dozen times back to back, stopping only briefly when Ryse makes an appearance, yelling and screaming about Esta and how Junco went and fucked it all up again. I have to push him outside and take him down on the cement to make him shut up.

HOUSE sleeps right through the whole debacle, right through till morning to be precise, and I'm left wondering if that's normal. Don't kids wake easily? Isn't that something parents are forever complaining about? Shushing visitors into whispers so the kids don't wake up?

And I can totally see why they want them sleepin'. Just the one little mouth exhausts me. I cannot even fathom people having *broods* of them at the same time.

Or what it's like to be a Clutch Mother.

That thought physically makes me shudder.

I'm about to start the loop again when I see him out on the terrace. His hair more blond than it was last time. His clothes fitting right in with our tropical location, like he really was on a beach in Australia a few minutes ago.

I'm outside—my razors out, my fangs protruding—as I storm up to him. "You better have some answers for me." It takes every ounce of control I have not to start the brawl no questions asked.

Gideon smiles and starts to circle me. "Ya know I don't owe you any answers, Beast."

I cringe at the name. HOUSE called me that, too. The whole world is calling me that now. "Where's Caleb?" I ask, probing for information.

Gideon laughs. "Too busy to bother with you, that's for sure. If you've got a message you can give it to me. I'll see that he gets it."

My eyes burn into him as I let the revelation sink in. "It fits ya, you know? If that's the job He gave ya. Yer no Messenger, yer nothing but a delivery boy."

We continue to circle, his eyes shifting briefly towards the terrace door, then back to me. "And what does that makes you, an Angel?"

I growl at this accusation. "Say it again, Gideon, and I'll rip that pretty-boy head right off yer body. Let's see how well they put ya back together then."

He stops his circling and draws himself up to his full height. He's got like two centimeters on me but he acts like it's some insurmountable distance that proves he's superior.

I stay in my ready position.

"I just came to tell you that Sera's in there with her."

"And? That's supposed to make me feel better? You set her up to be dissipated, Gideon. You stupid. Mother. Fucking. Piece of shit." The words come out low and even. I don't lose my temper often, preferring to handle things calmly whenever possible because of the consequences, but this guy pushes my buttons like he's taking lessons from Annun.

He watches me for a sign of attack before answering. "Yeah, and she agreed to it, Tier. I might give her orders, and she might follow them most of the time. But we both know, Junco is about as unpredictable as they come. I have no more sway over her than you—"

I tackle him—straight in the chest. He goes flying backwards and we crash onto the cement. I can feel the breath as it gets knocked out of him and then his hands are around my throat, squeezing until I start to choke. I ignore that and send my claws scraping across his face. His skin opens up in long gashes that spew blood and his hands release from my neck just before the stars start closing in.

I back up and get to my feet, then watch him circle me. Blood is still dripping down his cheeks, but not as bad as it was a few seconds ago.

I nod at him, breathing heavy as I recover from oxygen loss. "That's some trick then, eh? You got that self-healing gene how, Gideon? Because from what I know of yer background, yer not supposed ta have that. You were never Aves, were ya?"

He lets out a small laugh between breaths, but it's not nearly as cocky as it was a few minutes ago. "Says who?"

"Says Junco. She told me you skipped a very important life stage. Never had wings, did ya? Ya felt her all up when she was back at Subjack's, she said, and you had no clue what you were doing. Which means you've never even spent time with a true avian, only those worthless clones they got out there in the MR. Ya have no experience with wings, right? That's what ya told her?"

His silence says I'm on to something, I'm just not sure what it is yet.

"Whose team are you playing for, Gideon? Quit yer bullshit, OK? I already know yer not him, so just tell me who ya are and we'll be good."

He laughs for real now and it has me recalculating on the fly. "Not who? Not Gideon? Oh, shit! That's what you think?"

It's my turn to be quiet and listen.

"Fuck! I thought you really *were* on to me, but this is priceless!" He shakes his head. "Not Gideon! That's awesome." His mood changes from amused to rage in an instant and I feel every molecule of adrenaline in my body as it's shunted to my major muscle groups.

He stalks up to me, pushes his chest right against me, and his eyes rage red as they bore into mine. "I'm Gideon, Tier. I'm the only fucking Gideon there is." His words come out low, both in character and volume. They rumble from his throat like a snarling nightdog—a voice that could match Lucan on his worst days. "And if you told Junco this lie to make her doubt me, I will make you pay, *brother.* Because I'll put up with a lot from you, but I will not put up with you fucking up what she and I have."

He turns and walks back a few paces, stops and breathes deeply for a few moments, then pivots back to face me again.

"But even if you did tell her that bullshit, then obviously she didn't believe you, because she did what I told her to do, and she did it willingly."

"Yeah, she got herself dissipated into the nether," I say calmly. "That was yer grand plan? To have her kill herself. Again?" He takes a breath and I know instantly that was definitely not the plan. "What *was* the plan, Gideon? Because it's about as fucked up as it can get right now. She's as good as dead, you asshole! She's as good as dead!"

His smile is back, like that throaty demonic voice never happened. "This plan is not fucked up. Derailed, slightly, yes. I concede that. But as I was saying, Sera— "

"I don't want to die."

I whirl at HOUSE's terrified voice behind me and walk over and put a hand on her back, pushing her away. "Yer not gonna die, darlin'. Just go back inside."

"What the fuck is that?" Gideon demands. "You have one of those clones?" He looks at me with an air of incredulous repulsion. "Man, I always knew you were sick, but this! Sick!"

He drops his words, like he can't even think straight. And it hits me then. He has no idea who this child is, he thinks I'm keeping a little baby Junco for fuck's sake.

I look back at HOUSE and she's staring at him, but she makes no move to straighten out the misunderstanding.

My head swivels to Gideon and he's backing away from us. "You're sick, Tier." And then he disappears. Which is yet another talent he shouldn't have access to.

I rub my face in exhaustion as I start adding up all the facts about Gideon that I can count on to be true. He's a lone Seven, we're pretty sure that's true. He came from the Stag. He was raised and trained with Junco. He told her fairy tales that are not part of this world. He was taken away in his teens and morphed into *something*. He's got open Archer marks so he's never been claimed, by anyone. He was never avian, let alone Aves, yet he can port and heal. He spent a fair amount of time with Inanna, this he told me himself while Junco was in her Archer morph. He's definitely still sleeping with that Iliana Seven clone, or whatever she is nowadays. And he claims to knows Caleb well enough to have access.

It's the last part that worries me, although the idea that Gideon and I have shared a girlfriend, even if she was in two totally different bodies, is enough to make me retch.

Fucking Iliana. I must've been out of my mind that year.

The smacking of flipflops pulls me back from my thoughts. HOUSE slides up next to me and wraps her little fingers around my hand as she stares at the empty space where Gideon disappeared. "What do you think Junco sees in him?"

I look down at her wide eyes. They shine yellow in the early morning sunlight and I smile. "I have no idea, darlin', but I think you deserve a trip to the beach just for asking that question."

Chapter Five

The promise of a day at the beach keeps HOUSE busy making preparations while I spend the time rewinding my short conversation with Gideon over and over in my head, but there is nothing really new there. We all *think* we know who Gideon is working for, but Caleb has only shown himself once as far as I know. And I only know about that because Junco told Lucan during an argument and Lucan shared it with me.

And once we make it down to the beach it just feels wrong, somehow, to be lounging in an inner Sargassum cabana after Junco was smashed to particles inside that Pillar. But the truth of the matter is, I have very little to do without a completed Pillar Seven.

I watch HOUSE jump back from the waves down near the water and some of the heaviness in my chest lifts. Just slightly. I have to admit, I am enjoying Junco's HOUSE. I might even like her. Besides, I get the feeling HOUSE has a distaste for Gideon, and that makes me more amicable in putting up with her escapades.

Of which there were many today.

First, she spent most of the morning choosing a bathing suit. It's currently a one-piece—we fought about that for the better part of an hour and still she had a two-piece delivered via the automated shop tubes and tried to put it on with a t-shirt over it, like she's the most clever child who walks the Earth and I'm just some dumb winged fool who doesn't know any better. And then she states we *have* to pack up a cool sack with drink pouches and peanut butter and jelly sandwiches on oat bread and *then* she refuses to let me port us to the beach, insisting that all the families she's watched on screen have to lug their crap to the sea in misery and make it a big production.

So I had to haul all this shit—towels, lotion, cool sack, and various plastic building tools and accessories—down the elevators and out to the beach cabanas, like a human. But the kicker of the morning was when she insisted I wear swim trunks. I gave in when she threw in the sunglasses. I feel like I'm living out some Rural Republic husband's vacation nightmare.

Lucan ports in waving his hands and talking non-stop. I set my beer down in the sand—the only good thing coming out of this day—and wait for him to finish.

He eyes the various seating accommodations and sets himself in the white linen sling chair, then notices me for the first time and points to my clothes. "What is that?"

"Beach wear."

He searches for HOUSE, who is down at the edge of the beach filling several orange pails with water, and then directs his gaze back to me. "She's still here." It's a statement, not a question.

"Yup, she's still here."

"What are you doing, Raubtier?"

I shrug. "She's Junco's HOUSE, little sister if I believe the kid. Junco asked me to take care of her, what am I supposed ta do? Drop her off somewhere and leave?"

He sighs. "They've located Gideon, he's at Subjack's compound in the Polar Friendly."

"I know. Well, I know he was found because he showed up here."

"He's telling everyone who will listen that you're keeping a baby Junco clone as a pet."

I take a swig of beer and swallow before replying. "Did ya correct them?"

"No. I found it too absurd to acknowledge."

"You wanna hear something funny?" I crack a smile and wait for him to agree.

He rolls his hand at me to get on with it.

"They don't know this little sister HOUSE exists. No one knows. It's like she's Junco's last secret or something. She never told anyone, Lucan. Not even Gideon or her father."

He watches the girl for a few moments as I watch him. Then I take my gaze to the child as well. "Secrets, when it comes to Junco, are a pretty big deal. Why would she keep this AI being a secret? Her father must know, how could he not?"

Lucan's still watching HOUSE when he answers. "He doesn't though, he called me and wanted to know if that clone rumor was true. If he knew, he wouldn't ask that." His face turns to me again. "Would he?"

A slow smile forms. "I feel like we've been handed a gift, Lucan. I'm not sure what it means, but it's big, I think."

"Maybe. Give me one of those, will you?" He points to my beer and I reach over to the cool sack and pull out a bottle and hand it over. He opens it with a crack of bursting air and takes a gulp.

HOUSE is chatting away busily as she approaches the cabana, dumps her pails of water out on the sand a few feet away from us, and then wipes her runny nose on her arm.

The sand splashes against Lucan's pristine black armor and I watch him scowl as he brushes it off.

I intervene before he can make a big deal out of it. "Why don't ya build yer castle in the wet sand, HOUSE? It's easier than dragging these pails of water up here."

"I don't like those ships out there," she says, pointing to the cabana roof.

"Those are our ships. It's just security."

She huffs. "They're not all that secure, if you ask me."

"Of course they're secure," Lucan replies with more patience than he did last time. He must figure there's something to my idea about HOUSE being Junco's secret. "They're impenetrable."

"Is that so?" HOUSE asks.

Lucan is about to answer in the affirmative when a plasma cannon fires, exploding several cabanas a few hundred yards down the beach.

"What the fuck was that!" I'm on my feet asking for clarification from the ships when HOUSE puts a hand over her mouth to stifle a giggle. I tell the ship to wait and scowl at her.

"Did you do that?"

She nods. "I told you they're not secure. It was easy. And if I can do it, then everyone can do it." She stops to look at Lucan. "Right?"

He reaches over and pats her on the head. "I think we've found our secret."

"What's that mean?" she asks.

Annun is standing in front of us, spewing out excuses before I even know what he's talking about. "Tier, I swear, we didn't do that! Arel has no idea—"

"Never mind," I cut him off. "Take HOUSE down to the water and help her build a sand castle."

He stares at me. "What the fuck is a sand castle?"

Sometimes this guy is so stupid. I have to keep reminding myself that he never did a hosting on Earth because he's totally clueless about human culture. "She'll show ya."

I turn to HOUSE. "Annun is a friend of Junco's, he'll watch ya so you can build down by the water, OK?"

She shrugs and begins bossing him around, telling him to take some pails and shovels, and then proceeds to drag him down to the water by the shirt. To his credit he follows and doesn't even balk. I watch her for several minutes, smiling, before I realize that I'm still standing in the middle of the cabana.

"You're a natural, Tier."

I look over a Lucan as I take my seat and grab my beer again. "A natural at what?"

"Fatherhood," he says. "It suits you. Really, it does. It comes easy. Not like me." He stops and I figure we're both thinking about his attempts at parenting.

I laugh a little to myself.

"What's funny?"

"Ya weren't *that* bad. I mean, we lived, right?"

"Is that the standard for a successful clutch? Survival?"

My brows twist at his question. "For avians? Uh, yeah, pretty much. Why? Yer human these days or something?"

"I just wonder, after hearing some of Junco's stories, if it's not a bit extreme."

"I don't get it. Her life was far worse than mine, so you were a better father than Subjack was, that's for sure."

"Was I? I could've saved you a lot of injuries, pain, and trouble if I wanted to."

"Yeah, and I'd have ended up as stupid and weak as ninety-five percent of the population of Earth, Lucan. Stop. We live the way we live for a reason. I'm not unhappy, I'm not scarred. I'm fine. Ashur's fine. Rikan's fine. We're all fine."

He takes another drink. "But tell me, wouldn't you rather have a quiet life with Junco and that AI child down there? Than fighting all the time?"

"What's this about?"

He eyes me for a few seconds and then turns away. "You could change your wishes, you know." He turns back. "And then it won't matter if she's been dissipated. Will it?"

"It's too late now, Lucan."

"Yes, but if we *win*." He stops again and stares into me. "If we win, Raubtier."

I look down the beach at HOUSE and watch her squeal and clap and jump. Arel is there now, helping them build, as well as several more avians from the ship, all with random tools, real honest-to-God avian tools, that move the wet sand around at HOUSE's direction.

"If we win, you could change."

"Maybe. But not is not the time to think about that shit. It's a nice day, this playing and relaxing. But Junco's still gone, the Pillar is still struggling to assemble, and the Halo is not in place. We've got about five days until they reach the Oort Cloud Gate and then we're pretty much fucked. So no more talk about wishes. Fuck the wishes, Lucan. They don't matter because none of us will be here if we can't figure out something fast. And even *with* that fucking Halo, our chances are slim. There's no way we can take them, none. We need a miracle if ya ask me, and from what I've seen, Caleb's boss is not interested this time."

He takes a long swig of his beer and sits quietly, watching the scene play out down by the water for a few minutes before adding anything to the conversation. "All true. But you're missing something these days, Tier, and it's got me worried."

"Yeah? What am I missing, Lucan?"

"Faith."

Annun walks into the cabana and interrupts our conversation. "Where's the food? That little monster wants some food." He smiles as he says it and I can't help myself, I crack one too. She is a little monster, that's for sure. I point to the cool pack. "In there."

He reaches in, pulls a sandwich out, takes a bite and chews.

I wait for it.

"It's good."

I can only laugh. They do grow on you, those disgusting little concoctions. Maybe it's the oat bread?

He takes a handful of sandwiches and some drink bags and heads back to the water. Lili is there now, and Ryse is barking out directions to the various warriors who are busy erecting a second story on the castle.

Lucan gets up abruptly and walks back towards the boardwalk near the buildings. "Walk with me, Tier," he calls over his shoulder.

I get up and follow him across the sand.

He stops at the cement path that winds its way around the edge of the atoll beach and waits for me to catch up. "Amelia is asking for me and Rikan is there as well, so—"

I sigh. "So yer going back to be with *them*, then?" I didn't mean for it to come out jaded, but it does.

"Yes," he says simply, and then puts both hands on my shoulders and stares into my eyes. "But I want you to know, Tier, that you were not the decoy, do you understand? You are not the decoy. In thousands of years of life, you were my one true choice and regardless of what Gib's genetic charts say, you are my one true son."

It almost stops my heart, this revelation. He's never said these words to me before.

"And no matter what happens, I love you and have enjoyed every moment of your upbringing. I wish I'd paid closer attention and kept you home more, to be honest. I missed a lot, I think."

I have no words for this, I just frown and try to hold myself together.

"And if we win—*when*—when we win, I want you to have the same opportunity. Just think about it. I know it's not how you imagined your life, but just think about it."

He drops his hands and I nod out a yes to his request. "I'll think about it."

He smiles and turns to leave instead of disappearing outright. "Will you be back?" I call out before he can make his exit.

"I will be back, Raubtier," he says. "But I will be back in chains."

And then he's gone.

I stand there, the warm tropical wind whipping past my face—half watching the warriors build a sand castle with Junco's HOUSE, half listening to her excited squeals—as I play his last words in my head, over and over again.

He's put it all on me.

Because right now I outrank every being on this planet. And even though at every formal introduction I've ever made—be it with Subjack, or Caleb, or the other alien leaders in the Polar Friendly—I've always declared that my words are Lucan's words, it's never felt real until now.

I am Lucan's one true son.

Chapter Six

I sit in the cabana alone for several hours, just watching the line of sand castles appear along the shore. HOUSE's castle was declared complete a while ago and they've since moved on to the other congregations of avian warriors who have found their way down to the Sargassum resort.

If Ashur sees them all down here fucking off he's gonna piss his pants.

HOUSE gave up and came back to the cabana about twenty minutes ago, stretching out on the sand floor and babbling about her castle, her sunburn, and her missing flipflop for a few minutes before passing out from exhaustion. Her body is sprawled out haphazardly, half on a large multi-colored beach towel and half off.

I'm on my seventeenth beer.

Junco's Pillar hasn't even grown a picometer for more than two hours. Arel pops in every now and then to update me with the bad news. We're off the timeline now. No hope, as far as he can tell.

Hopeless, in fact, was the word he used.

I close my eyes and just sit there, silent and still.

And that faith Lucan was harping on at me about? Well, fuck faith. It's got a whole lot to do with nothing, I figure.

Annun wanders in shuffling around for a beer in the cool sack that has long since lost its coldness. And its beer.

"They're gone," I declare from the shadows.

He turns abruptly and laughs. "Shit, dude! You scared me!" He watches me take a slow drink off the last of the warm beer and then shifts his weight with apprehension.

I know my eyes are glowing because I can see the shadows.

And I know they're not green because HOUSE's face is lit up red. It isn't from sunburn.

"You all right, Tier?"

I take another swallow of beer. "No, not really."

He takes a seat in the canvas chair to my left and eases himself back, kicking out his legs a little, like he's just relaxing with a friend.

"I had a heart-to-heart with Junco once. Did you know that? Back when we were in Fledge together."

My eyes drift back down to HOUSE's sleeping body. It's so fucking unfair that Junco can be so close and yet so far at the same time. It's so fucking unfair.

"Yeah," he continues. "We were both up in the Church the night of the Sixth Fight. Lucan let the 039 give us a party to celebrate and we went over there."

It's such a struggle to even exist at the moment.

"She played piano for us that night. It was beautiful, ya know?" He looks over to me and I can tell he's a little drunk as well. "I'd been watching her fight all those weeks and I'd already formed an opinion of her. In my mind she was like a fucking rabid dog or something." He stops to laugh. "I mean, she was crazy in the Third Fight. I saw her in the maze at one point, wielding that SEAR knife like some kind of ancient avian from the myths and I thought to myself, damn, that bitch is out of her mind scary!"

I smile at this, because she really is. I would not want to fight her and Ashur is damn lucky she didn't chop his head off when he attacked her back in Vegas.

"Anyway," Annun continues, slurring the word a bit. "We both ended up in the church that night and we got to talking about what it means to be a warrior. And she told me something that haunts me."

He stops and leans over with his head in his hands and my interests picks up. "Well, what'd she say?"

He looks up and his eyes are more bloodshot than I remember them being a second ago. "She said she likes who she is and what she can do. And she'd never choose to be anything else."

"Huh," is the only response I can manage to that thoroughly depressing nugget of news.

"And I've thought about that talk we had endlessly, it seems, since she was taken and all this shit's been going down. Because I don't think she meant it."

I toss my empty bottle into the pile and it clinks against the others. I check HOUSE to see if that woke her, but she's breathing heavy and deep with sleep. "And what makes you so sure that wasn't what she meant, Annun?" I drag my gaze over to him and watch him squirm again.

"Because she carried this little card around with her in Fledge. A prayer card from the church. I never did get a real good look at the one she had, she kept it tucked in her pants. But I saw the front of it once, so I went looking for that card in the Fledge Church after Inanna took her and you came home. And I found it."

He stops and lets the seconds drag on, forcing me to participate in the conversation. "What'd it say?"

His smile is weak when he begins to explain. "It was about destiny, about meeting destiny on your own terms, actually, and not just accepting it. So that was a message that was important to her, right? And that's why she carried the card. So when I think about what she said in that church that night, maybe it was just a little bit of her insanity coming out, and not the real her. Because if she believes she's the captain of her soul, then she can't be blindly sailing the winds of destiny too."

I close my eyes and hope.

"She gets lost sometimes, I think. And scared, ya know? And she does and says things that contradict her true self. So that's what I thought this whole dissipation thing was about at first, right? That she's lost in there right now, and she just needs a little help to find her way back. Like maybe she's more scared of what's waiting back here than she is up there, and she just needs someone to tell her it's OK. That's she's doing fine."

I grunt at this.

"But then I talked to HOUSE today and she also told me something."

Now this I want to hear, so I actually sit up in my chair. "What'd she say?"

He draws in a breath between his teeth and I can tell this is bad. I want to choke the life out of him right now but I force myself to be calm. "Go on, Annun. Just say it."

He shrugs. "Well, I was looking up at the sky and she caught me, thinking I was wondering about Junco, maybe. I wasn't, I was thinking about—"

"Just get on with it, Annun." I growl it this time and he nods.

"OK, yeah. She said, *She's not scared.* I asked her who and all that, trying to figure out what she's talking about, and she just said it again. She said, *Junco's not scared. She has a little bit of peace.*"

I grunt again. "Well, as Junco would say, that's fucking awesome."

Annun sighs at me. "Shit, dude, you're so clueless sometimes, ya know that? She's not scared, right? Which means she planned this. And HOUSE says she's at peace, which to me means she got to her end and couldn't take it any more. So the only thing to do when you get that far down the road, Tier, is just accept shit. And that, my dense superior officer, is exactly the right place for you to enter the picture."

"How do ya figure, Annun?"

"Because when you're ready to quit like that, you're really just begging for someone to come along and take charge, right? You just want to give it over to someone else." He shrugs and gets to his feet. "That's how I see it anyway. I watched her in Fledge. I saw her out there with you in Deliverance. And I figure I knew her better than anyone at that point in time. Maybe we didn't talk much, but I watched her very carefully. And I was her pick, ya know. I was her pick."

"I know, Annun. And that's why yer on my team right now."

"Yeah, well." He sucks in another breath. "This is your right place and your right time, Captain. All you gotta do is show up for the fucking party. Be the goddamned hero for once. Save Junco from herself because she's tired, Tier. She's had enough, she's been lied to, manipulated, scarred, mutated, cloned, killed, and tortured. And if I were her, I'd figure dissipation felt pretty motherfucking wonderful too. Better than any offer she's gotten here so far. Damned peaceful. She's definitely not coming back on her own. And maybe Sera's in there and maybe she's not, but you've got a direct link to Junco sleeping on the sand down there and all you've done today is drink beer. And maybe it's not my place to say it, but everyone else has been talking about it all day long, so fuck it—you can kick my ass if you want. Your kid's sick, Tier. Her nose is running, her head's all sweaty, and she's breathing like she needs a fucking respirator."

I sit up straight and ask my vision screen for an ethanol antagonist. It rushes into my blood stream and the lethargic drunk feeling is gone in an instant. "What?" I kneel down and pick her up and she whines in protest as I hold her to my chest. He's right, she's hot. "Shit, Annun. Why didn't ya say something earlier?"

"I have no experience with human kids, for fuck's sake, and you're the one taking care of her, not me. Everyone here but you can see she's not an AI, Tier. She's something else, so ya know… maybe you should try and figure that out and get your ass back to work before we all get blown to bits by the fucking Angels."

I wipe the sweat off her forehead and lean into her ear. "HOUSE?"

"Hmmm?" She squirms in my arms and swats my hand off her face.

"Ya OK, darlin'?"

"I'm tired," she mumbles, then turns into my chest and goes back to sleep.

I stand up and hold her tight. "She's tired."

"Yeah," Annun says. "Like I said. She's tired. Just save her from herself, dude. She just wants to rest."

Chapter Seven

The fires down below burn well into the night. Not out of any kind of celebration, but just as a way to stave off the darkness and impending doom, I think. I'm still not sure if Ashur gave the go-ahead for all these warriors to be here on the beach, but I figure they're none of my business anymore, so what the fuck do I care if they're not following orders?

I don't care.

They're just making the most out of the time we have left.

HOUSE is inside still asleep on the couch where I put her down more than two hours ago. I put in a call to Layla but she's not even on ship right now. So I found a medi-kit in the bathroom and gave her some medicine to cool her off and the last time I checked, it was working and this makes me feel a little less like a total piece of worthless shit.

I want to get drunk again very badly, but I let my metabolism clean up my blood and live with the consequences of my new reality. My head is hanging over the edge of the terrace in a sort of solitary pity party when Caleb ports in next to me.

I know he's there but I don't bother looking up.

"You're moping?" he asks.

"Yup," I reply, my forehead resting on my hands. "I'm fucking moping."

He walks behind me and takes a seat on the patio chair.

"Join me, Tier. I have a question for you."

My senses perk up at this, but I don't get too excited. It's Caleb, after all.

"What question? You wanna know why I'm keeping a baby Junco clone, too?"

"Is the rumor true, then?"

This makes me turn. "What?" I study him for a few seconds. He looks way too much like Gideon for my comfort level. He's got the same sandy blond hair, blue eyes, and all-around perfect guy persona going for him.

"*Do* you have a clone here? I've been told you paraded her around the beach this afternoon, is it true?"

How is this possible? That he, of all people, is not aware? How could this possibly be the best-kept secret in the Solar System? "Yeah, it's true," I say and then walk over and take the seat across from him because this is just way too interesting.

"We're not quite sure what to make of that, to be honest. Everyone thinks you've gone insane."

"I've never been accused of being sane, Caleb. You know me better than that."

"True," he says, averting his eyes to the door. I look as well, hoping like hell that HOUSE doesn't come out while we're talking.

I turn back. "Is that why you came? To assess my sanity?"

"No, I've come with a message, I said. We have an offer, if you're interested."

"Yeah? What's that, then?"

He studies me for a long time and I simply sit still under his gaze and study him back.

If someone asked me to describe how I am related to Caleb, I'd be at a loss for words. We are twins, but not. We are brothers, but not. We are friends, but not. We are the sanctioned sons of very powerful beings and have unimaginable abilities, but have no real clearance to wield it. Yet. Although he's always been sanctioned, I was only promoted to this position today.

"He is not happy with Lucan. Not at all. He allowed the summoning gift under conditions, Tier. Conditions that there would be no more. And then you two decided to allow Isten, of all people, to twine her mind. What the hell were you thinking?"

I raise my eyebrows and make to answer but he waves me off.

"Never mind, it was rhetorical. But then Inanna marked her with the Archer morph. But that mark is Lucan's, you are aware, correct?"

"Of course it's Lucan's mark. Inanna has no authority to mark for herself."

"She was not Lucan's, Tier. We are not happy about this development. In fact, I'd go so far as to say He is extremely pissed off. I've never seen him so angry."

"She's always been one of ours, Caleb. She came straight from Gyr."

"No, you're wrong. She is His, Tier. She came straight from Him and He is not happy."

Huh. So there it is. The confirmation I've been looking for. She was made by Him.

"I said," he enunciates, "He is not happy, Tier. You owe us now. A soul for a soul."

I grunt out a laugh. "You have three of my brothers, Caleb. You've gotten more than your share."

"We never wanted them, you know that, Tier. We had to take them because they were left unmarked by Lucan. Their gifts were sanctioned and we had no choice. So that is why we took Selia. She is the only pure thing you had to offer. But this unsanctioned claim will not be forgiven."

I've lost all my patience. "Who gives a shit, anyway? Do you think I give a fucking shit? She's fucking *gone*, Caleb!"

I take a very deep breath to bring the claws back in.

"I could intervene in this one instance. But we will take Junco afterward. I'd need Lucan's permission of course."

"Ah, you lowly piece of shit!" I point at him. "You know damn well I have the baby Junco, right? Because you were listening to my conversation with Lucan earlier. And now you know I *am* the sanctioned son. And you know Lucan wants Junco. Yet maybe you can persuade me to speak for him and give her up, is that why you're here?"

He holds his words.

"Fuck you." I get up and go back to the terrace wall and look down the beach again. "Fuck. You."

He joins me and starts his speech in a whisper. "We don't need your permission, Tier. Gideon has a claim, as do Subjack and Inanna. We could get her any of these other three ways."

"So take her." I turn and lean back on the railing, satisfied with my positioning for the first time in a very long time. "Take her if you can get her."

"She's stuck in the Pillar."

"Yeah, that was your man Gid's idea. And you think he's on your team?" I laugh.

"They've got a private agenda, those two. They're not playing by the rules."

I let out a long, loud laugh at this. "Really? Well, fuck. Who would've thought that Gid and Junco might have their own fucking plan? Huh? Who'd a thought that after more than two decades of bullshit, torture, and psychological damage that they might want some motherfucking revenge? Where the fuck have you been for the last twenty-two years, asshole? Where the fuck has *He* been?"

"You know the rules about interference."

I stare at him in a rage, my eyes lighting up the whole terrace. "Who is Gideon? Is he yours?" A small shake of the head is all I get, but I push. "Then who the fuck does he belong to?"

"He belongs to no one," Caleb starts, "for now."

"He's an Archer, Caleb. How the hell can he not be claimed?"

Silence.

"I know Inanna did his morph because Lucan sure as hell didn't. And if Inanna did his morph, then he'd be Lucan's warrior. And his scars are not Lucan's."

"Why not ask your father who he belongs to? Why me?"

"Because I know he's yours, asshole. What I don't know is how he managed to do that when Inanna's the one who morphed him."

"Gideon is special. He's a Seven, he's a Warrior, he's Saved, he's just special. And that's all you'll get out of me because it is against the rules to—"

"Against the *rules*?" I laugh so loud a few people down below actually look up at the apartment building. "Get the fuck off my terrace. In fact, get the fuck off my Goddamned island. My motherfucking planet. Do you hear me? Get the fuck out of my universe, you pathetic weaseling piece of shit. You think you can play innocent and blame this whole fucking mess on *rules*?"

His scowl is a warning that I respond to with fangs and knives.

"I'm not giving Junco up, how about that? Gideon won't give her up either, nor will Subjack, and even if Inanna wasn't stuck in the Pillar with her she'd want something in return, and we both know she's not getting that! I know all of this with one hundred percent certainty. I'm yer last resort, aren't I? Ya can't even find Gideon, I bet. We'll I'll make it easy for ya. He's up in the Polar Friendly, go ask *him* for permission."

I turn back to the sea and continue scanning the beach.

"Raubtier—"

"Don't," I growl. "Don't you fucking dare use my given name. I'll swipe that pretty face off yer body if ya say it again."

"What are they doing up there in the Polar Friendly? You ever wonder that?"

"Who gives a shit?"

"All those people up there do, for starters. Subjack is there, Carolinia Coot is there as well. Gideon, all the alien leaders who've made their way to Earth over the centuries. And you never asked yourself, why? You've never allowed yourself the luxury of asking why the High Order comes to this planet? Of all the billions, trillions of habitable planets in this Universe, why the *fuck* would they want this stupid little planet that has no hospitable neighbors for twenty standard light years in all directions? Why here? And why do the aliens congregate in the Arctic?"

"Why are they up there, then? Huh? I'm not in the mood to play games with you tonight, Caleb. If you're trying to make a point, then make it."

He smiles. "Well, see, here's the problem. This information is the actual message I was sent to offer. But I need a favor in return."

"I already told ya, I'm not handing her—"

"No, we already knew you'd never agree. Junco has been soiled with all sorts of Angel filth, we don't even want her."

I punch him in the face and he crashes to the ground. I'm about to slash through his torso with demon claws when he finally get to the point.

"I just need a minute with her when she comes out of the Pillar, that's all. We won't take her. Can't take her. But she's being very difficult, and you should know she said some disturbing things during my last approach."

I'm almost afraid to ask, after hearing Annun's earlier confession about how she loves who she is, but I can't help myself. "What'd she say?"

"That she wants to die. So she can see Isten again."

I cringe at the name. Isten was a huge mistake. I never thought she'd go insane like this over it. We've misjudged her so many times it's pitiful.

"I didn't tell her that she's never crossing the Bridge, Tier. I didn't tell her, couldn't bear to tell her. She was truly a pathetic mess."

"Lucan broke the news. She already knows the truth."

"Good, good," he muses. "But it's such a shame that your soul is still unclaimed, isn't it? What with the impending apocalypse and your death all but assured. You probably figured you'd cross together one day, right? But now she's been turned and claimed and you wasted the last two years taking orders from the Devil."

My eyes close for an exaggerated moment. "It is what it is, Caleb. Destiny is a total fucking bitch." He gets to his feet and I step back to give him some room.

"But it doesn't have to be. I could step in and make adjustments."

I don't even hesitate. "No, thanks."

"So you'll give her to Lucan? For eternity?"

The heat overtakes my body and forces me to take another deep breath to prevent the turn. "Why are you here?"

He leans back on the terrace railing, cool again. Assured in his position. "I told you, a single minute of her time after you pull her out of the Pillar."

"Why?"

He shakes his head. "None of your business. If she wants to tell you after, that's her prerogative, but you will not get that information from me."

"And you'll give me what?"

"I'll give you to Lucan."

"I'm already Lucan's."

"Not officially. You need the Archer morph for that. But I can step in."

"You want me to allow you to ban me!" I laugh, it's so absurd. "I am the sanctioned son! I have immunity! If I wanted to stay here, Caleb, I'd give myself to my *father*, not let *yours* ban me like a common criminal."

He sighs, like I'm boring the shit out of him. "Why do I care? Huh? Why do we care what happens here in this universe? Do you ever ask yourself any questions at all, Tier?"

"You care because you know the High Order will cross that Bridge one day. And your Almighty Father isn't as powerful as He makes Himself out to be. You care because you're just as afraid of them as we are."

I admit, I was reaching when I said the words but his silence says I'm right.

And this sucks.

Because if they really are afraid of the High Order then we're all fucked.

"Will you ask Him to help us?" I ask.

"Will you stay here and give up your position?"

"It's tempting, I'll admit that, but if I'm not ready to sell my soul at Lucan's request, you can damn well be sure I'm not gonna do it for you."

"Oh!" he says with amusement. "Forgive me, I thought you'd be giving your soul to Lucan at Junco's request. That's the only reason you'd do the morph, right? To stay with her forever? But maybe I misjudged your attachment to her? I apologize for jumping to conclusions. I figured this was an easy win on my part. That you actually might care about someone other than yourself and that father of yours. My mistake."

"You know damn well it's not that easy, so don't make it sound like I'm a total piece of shit because I'm hesitant to give up my own personal salvation."

"Right. Salvation. Tier, let's not live in fantasy land, OK? You're not salvageable, brother. You'd be allowed to cross over on a technicality *only* and the thought of you living in our world makes me sick. Your soul might pass on, but you'd never be saved. Why not just stay here in the world of the damned and be happy with your lot in life?"

"It might take a while to wash the blood off, friend, but eventually the water will run clear. You and I both know eternity is a very long time. I'm not worried about it."

"So we're back to my original question. You'll leave her here alone, for Lucan to use as he sees fit? For eternity?"

He sighs when I refuse to answer. "Fine, have it your way. If you give me one minute alone with her after she's removed from the Pillar, I'll provide you with some information. To aid your efforts in resisting your forefathers."

My laugh almost comes out as a snort. "What information could you possibly have about this world?"

"They're digging up there in the Polar Friendly, Tier. And they've found things. They've found some very interesting things. Several very interesting things, brother."

I wait it out since he's feeling chatty.

"Haven't you wondered where the Seven Siblings came from? After thousands of years, all of a sudden these genetics just appear? You never wondered?"

"Of course I've wondered."

"A minute with her, after you get her out of the Pillar. Just a minute. Sixty seconds, that's all I need. You can time us."

"And you'll get her out, too?"

He laughs. "No, that's your problem. But I have faith in you, Tier. I'm not worried about it."

I think about this. It's a welcome sign, really. My shoulders relax and I let out a breath.

"One minute. And I'll tell you what's in that pit they're digging up there."

"I could just go ask Subjack, I don't need yer information."

"You do that, then. Good luck, because he hates you. You want his only daughter and I can certainly relate to how a father might feel about *that* little familial arrangement. Plus, you've gone insane. I'm not sure why you're keeping that clone, but it's quite possibly the most disturbing thing I've ever witnessed."

I grunt. *Right.*

"One minute."

"Fine, sixty seconds, *after* I make sure she's OK."

I expect him to say *wonderful!* or *excellent!* like he usually does, but he hesitates, and then begins to talk in a low voice. "You know how I always knew it would be you in the end?"

"What?" That was a twist I never expected.

"I always knew it was you, Tier. Not Ashur, not Rikan, even though he is Lucan's genetic son. It was always you."

I watch his eyes carefully as the conversation turns to me. "I cannot even fathom the ego it must take to think ya always knew that answer, Caleb."

He smiles, but it's not a mean smile. Not even a boasting smile.

"I always knew it was you because when he brought you to the Bridge as a child for those early meetings he always held your hand, but he *never* held Ashur's hand. Or even Rikan, when he came later and was still young enough to be afraid. I saw each of you make that walk and I noticed this difference right away. At first I thought it was because you were scared or nervous, but you were never afraid, were you, Tier? You always wanted to cross the Bridge."

I swallow at the memories of being led up there. To meet and bond with my opposite and then later, to get the sanctioned gifts from Caleb's father. My brothers have all made that trip many times in the past two years. Many times to get many sanctioned gifts. But not me. Every year when Ashur and I were small we'd go up with Lucan. Separately, which is why Caleb could make the comparisons, I guess. But I haven't been up there since I was five because all of my gifts since then have been illegal. Caleb is quite right—I'm the dirtiest motherfucking avian there is in this Solar System right now. Redemption is only mine on a technicality.

I called his father the anti-Lucan because even today, I have no idea what His name is. He is Him, or He, and that's about it. And to Ashur and I, Caleb was always the anti-chosen. Because we never knew which one of us would be the sanctioned son. I always figured it was gonna be Ashur, he's such a rules guy and always pretty much did what he was told. I almost never followed orders, and Rikan didn't come along until much later. We never even knew about him until Fledge.

That was the deal Lucan made with Him. He'd do His bidding, he'd flood the planet, kill the slaves, drive away the Angels, and take the curse and the punishments. But in the end, Lucan's one true son would be saved as a form of payment. And today he gave that salvation to me. I am the one true son. I am the one he would keep safe above all others.

Because I am the one, above all others, who needs that salvation right now. Junco thinks her past is dirty but compared to my future, the terrible things she's done are like freshly washed sheets drying in the wind.

I look back at Caleb and he's got his eyebrows raised, waiting to see if I'm interested in knowing how he had it all figured out.

I am.

"Why did he hold my hand?"

"Because he didn't want to let you go, brother." Caleb's voice is so soft I can barely make out the words. "The mere thought terrifies him, Raubtier. He clings to you like you are the most precious thing in this Universe."

I have no words for the second time today.

"He loves you, Tier. And he'll give you up to save you. But you'd be doing everyone a favor—yourself, us, Junco, and Lucan—if you'd just accept your place here in this world and be satisfied."

"Enough of this bullshit," I growl. "Just tell me what's up there in the ice!"

He lets out a long breath which sounds a lot like exasperation. "Whatever you say. Everything is up there, Tier. Everything." And then he disappears.

Everything? What the hell does that mean? "Deal's off, asshole," I yell to the sky. "That answer is not even worth six seconds!"

I go back inside and check on HOUSE. She's still a little hot but doesn't seem any worse. I lie down on the opposite couch, finally exhausted. It's been four days since I've had sleep and I hate to admit it, but Caleb has eased my mind in a way no one else could. He believes Junco will return.

And if he believes it, is basing future actions on it, then he's already seen it.

My faith is back.

And I've poured it all into Caleb's request because my anti-brother, of all people, has faith in *me*.

Sleep comes easy.

Chapter Eight

HOUSE is chatty and busy in the morning. She makes me breakfast from the autocook, blueberry pancakes, and we eat them out on the terrace.

"Ya feelin' better today, HOUSE?"

She itches her nose as she chews, rubbing snot all over her face, and then speaks with her mouth full. "Yeth."

I can totally see why people have kids now. She's pretty damn cute. "Well, I have the doctor coming anyway, just ta make sure." Regardless of what she says, she doesn't look better at all. She's still flushed, her nose is practically dripping, and her chest is starting to make a strange sound when she exhales.

She ignores my comment about the doctor and shovels more pancakes in her mouth. At least her appetite is good.

"So, have ya talked to Junco, HOUSE? Since she's been in the Pillar?" There's no real easy way to approach this subject, so fuck it. Might as well just be direct.

"Uh-uh," she says again with her mouth full, but I can't really tell if that was a yes or a no. A few more chews and a swallow later and she's ready to give it another try. "No, I can't talk to Junco. She's far away now. But I can feel her."

I eat some pancakes, trying not to get too excited, and wait to see if she continues on her own. It takes a few more bites of food, but she eventually has more to say.

"She's at peace, ya know."

"Yeah?" I ask. "So she doesn't want to come home?"

"Nope. I asked her to, though." She looks up at me with her large eyes and stops her fork midway to her mouth. "I did ask her, Tier, after she said that. But she didn't answer."

"Do ya think we could convince her to come home, if we tried real hard?" I swirl my pancakes in some syrup. "I mean, she likes us, right? Maybe she'd come back for us?"

HOUSE just shrugs and I drop it because Ryse ports in.

"Inside," I tell Ryse. He follows me into the apartment and I close the terrace door so HOUSE can't hear. "Did ya find Layla?"

"Yeah, she's doing rounds on the morph ship, she can't get here until later. We've got more than a hundred thousand avians in morph right now, so she's a little busy. Can't you get a doctor here for the kid?"

"She's not a kid, Ryse. She's—well fuck, I'm not sure what she is, but—"

"She's an AI, Tier. Get a fucking engineer already. I'm not sure why she can eat and sleep and all that human shit, but the fact remains, she was nothing but circuits and electrons back at Junco's place."

I glare at him but he doesn't retract his words. "Say what's on yer mind, Ryse, because I'm losing patience with ya."

"Get a grip on yourself, Tier. Junco's gone, but we're still here. We've got two billion people waiting to disembark the ships, four billion more on their way here, an incomplete Pillar Seven, no Halo, and all you can think about is the health status of that thing you're feeding breakfast to? Esta is fucking gone as well, in case you haven't noticed, Selia is all shot to hell, Ashur's been given control over the Warriors, and now Lucan's back on Amelia waiting to meet seven thousand years of planned retribution. I'm fucking sick of your shit. Pull yourself together."

"Ryse," I start calmly, "Junco's in the fucking Pillar, too, so don't—"

"Yeah, but the whole reason Esta went into the Pillar was because Junco said she'd be fine! She trusted her! I trusted her! Fuck! I trusted you too, and look how fucking far that got me!"

"Look, brother. We're all wound up right now, I get it, but yelling at me isn't gonna make it better. So just calm down."

He walks away, breathing hard, then pivots on his heel and the rage seeps out of his eyes as light. "You're sitting up here with that kid doing what?"

I look outside and see HOUSE watching us through the terrace doors. "Planning, Ryse. She's got a part to play and I'm just trying ta figure—"

"What the fuck are you talking about, Tier? Fuck her! You do realize this fucking baby Junco has put all our potential allies on hold, right?"

I just stare out at HOUSE.

"Fuck it. Forget it, OK? I'll go tell Ashur to call a meeting with the Friendlies up north, because I don't even think you could handle it right now. We're losing, Tier!"

"Wait!" I command before he can leave. "I'll take care of the Friendlies, OK? Tell Ash to go ahead with the migration and I'll take care of the Friendlies. Just give me one more day."

He doesn't even acknowledge me, just ports out and leaves me there feeling sorta stupid but not really caring. I can almost see the pattern here. It's like the whole puzzle is spread out before me, almost making sense, just a few mismatched pieces, just a few that are still askew and don't fit. But it's all right there, I just need to look at it from a new angle or something. Dig a little deeper.

Chapter Nine

"So, tell me again how it happened?"

HOUSE is playing with some dolls that came out of the auto-shopper and I'm kneeling on the floor in front of her. She's told me the story several times now, but it makes no sense.

"No." She scowls at me and goes back to her dolls.

"Subjack—"

"Commander Coot." She corrects me.

"Right." I'm failing to see the difference between the two, but for some reason, this is a point she will not concede. Commander Coot and Subjack are not the same person when she tells this story, even though she does admit they *are* the same person in real life. "Commander Coot reprogrammed your permissions and gave Junco full authority over you when she was ten."

"Almost ten," she corrects again.

"Does it matter, HOUSE? This bullshit with Commander Coot's name and Junco's exact age? Because—"

"You should not talk to me that way."

"Yer making me angry, *girl.*"

She goes back to playing.

I close my eyes and ask for patience. "One more time, OK? Junco was given permission and the two of ya discussed you having a holographic body, and then Junco asked ya to make a body, but forgot to add that it should be a holographic one, and then ordered ya to keep it a secret?"

"Yes," she says and then produces a cough so thick with mucus it makes me clear my throat and swallow. Layla's last message said she'd be here in a few hours, and that was more than a few hours ago.

"And yer real? I mean, what's inside ya?" I wait but she doesn't answer. "HOUSE?" No answer. "Is this part of the secret?"

She looks up at me, her eyes all watery with sickness and her face flushed with fever, and nods. "It's a secret."

"Don't you think Junco would want you to tell *me*, though? I mean, she told me to take care of ya, darlin'. And how can I take care of ya if yer sick and ya can't tell me the things I need to make ya better?"

She shrugs and goes back to dressing her dolls, her little fingers deftly pulling on a glittery rhinestone jacket, and then she shoves a pair of pink sunglasses on the doll's face. "I might be able to tell you something else." Her hazel eyes are glowing a bright yellow now, she's lit up like the sun. "I was sick once before." She stops to cough here and it makes me want to choke just listening to it, that's how filled with mucus she is—like her lungs are drowning in it. "Inanna took me to the doctor once. When Junco was very sick," she whispers.

Inanna! "Who?" I ask, my heart beating wildly.

"Inanna." She stops to cough and I wince and shake my head.

She's getting worse by the second and there is no time to figure out why Inanna is involved. "Tell me where she took ya, darlin'."

She stands up suddenly and falls against my chest burying her head, still coughing like crazy. "I don't feel well," she whimpers. "I'm sick again and that means Junco's dying."

Her body goes soft and limp and I have to reposition her so she doesn't slump to the floor. "HOUSE?" Shit. I pull her head back and her eyes are closed. "HOUSE? Tell me, where did Inanna take you?"

I shake her a little and she finally responds with a cough. "HOUSE?" Dammit! "HOUSE?"

"The Sagitta Building." She breathes out the words in an almost inaudible whisper.

Her coughing takes on a whole new level. I stand up, clutching her close and pacing the floor as the puzzle pieces start to fit into place. Dallas. The Sagitta Building is in Dallas. That's where John Hando took Junco the last time she worked with him. But she told me that it's not really a building, it's a giant transmitter used to send messages into space as well as the home to the only AI duality on the planet.

I locate Annun in another Sargassum building down the beach and transport us to his apartment. He's in the middle of taking a bite out of what might be a peanut butter and jelly sandwich when I scare the shit out of him.

"Whoa! Dude! You—"

He sees HOUSE in my arms, limp and pretty much unconscious, and checks himself.

"I need to see John Hando, right now. We need to get to the Sagitta Building and I know for a fact he's got access."

Annun nods but his eyes are trained on the drooping body in my arms and I see the panic. "Hando, Annun! NOW!"

"Right. I have the compound coordinates, should I—"

I steal them right out of his mind and port the three of us to the Dallas Underbelly.

Chapter Ten

"Which place is his?" I look around and see nothing but lifeless buildings. There are enough hanging trains attached to the underside of Upper Dallas to create a roar of noise and a constant vibration below my boots, but there are no trains above us because most of these old buildings reach up and connect directly to the underbelly. They are awash with filth and the occasional flashing of a half-lit neon sign creates a disturbing vertigo effect. The one across from us says Bail Bonds.

"That one is the main entrance," Annun says as he points to the sign. "They own about twelve city blocks from ground to ceiling. You can't tell from out here, but it's a total military complex inside these buildings."

"How do ya know that?"

He shoots me a dirty look. "It's my fucking job to know, asshole. What do you think I do around here, for fuck's sake?"

I tuck away his insubordination to deal with later. "How do we get in then, genius?" HOUSE stirs in my arms and I lean down to whisper. "Hold on, darlin'. We're almost there."

"We ring the bell." He waits for an oncoming grav bike to pass us and then leads the way across the street. We stop in front of a shoddy gate and Annun pushes a small white button on the side of a box that is affixed to the metal.

No one comes.

"Buzz it again." I order.

"No," he shoots back. "You ring once and then you wait."

I push his worthless ass out of the way and lay on the buzzer non-stop for a solid thirty seconds. Then punch it over and over for good measure.

I'm still punching when a crackle of voices can be heard in between my requests for attention.

I let up on the buzzer so they can talk.

"You are being tracked with plasma cannons, Beast. State your business."

"I need John Hando, right now." I try not to growl it, but HOUSE's breathing is getting more labored by the second. "I need John Hando!"

There's several seconds of silence and then another voice. "Who sent you?"

"Junco," comes out automatically. "Junco sent me and I need access to the Sagitta Building, immediately!"

I hear laughter on the other end and I'm about to blow when the voice comes back. "What's wrong with HOUSE?"

I guess we know who really holds Junco's secrets. "She's sick, she needs help and from what I've been told that help is located in the Sagitta Building. I know you have access, Junco told me. I know there's a dual AI in there, Junco told me. And I know that this HOUSE AI has been there at least once before, so I'm asking ya, if ya ever cared for the girl, please give me access."

The crappy piece of tech crackles one more time. "Step back across the street. I'll come out."

We wait for what seems like an endless string of long-drawn-out hours but when I check my vision screen it's only been a little over two and half minutes.

There's a rumble of a roll-up steel security door down the street and both Annun and I crane our necks to get a better look.

A fully stocked military vehicle pulls out, then slowly approaches us. Annun walks out towards the curb as it pulls up and six men jump out, all targeting him. He stands still as they search and I wonder for a moment if I should reevaluate my opinion of this impetuous asshole who reminds me way too much of Braun.

Hando comes to do the honors for me. He pats me down, but I have no weapons. I haven't needed weapons for more than ten years now. "Thank you," I say simply.

He doesn't respond, simply waves us to get in the truck. Only Hando and the driver comes with us, the rest of the men jog down the street and go back inside the compound the same way they came out.

Annun gets in and stretches out his legs like the Texican Mafia picks him up on a street corner every day of the fucking week and I reverse my almost higher opinion of him.

Hando lets me settle with HOUSE and then leans over and whispers in her ear. She stirs and tries to open her eyes.

"Ya know who she is, then?" I ask.

He leans back in his seat and nods. "I know. I was there the last time she got sick." His look, when he finds my eyes, is challenging. I'm not really sure what I expected the one Junco regrets getting away to be like, but it certainly wasn't this man sitting across from me right now. That he's a pureblood Texican is apparent by his long black hair, his brown skin, and the infamous eyes that look like deep, endless pits. But if I hadn't just visited the familial compound, I'd never peg him for mafia. He's got a pair of dark sunglasses riding high on his forehead looking like they very badly want to slip down his face, a pair of long tan shorts that have lots of pockets, a white t-shirt that states something very rude in Spanish, and sneakers that look like he stole them off a Utopian surfer.

"So ya met Inanna, then?" is all I can think of to say.

Hando nods. "Yes. I knew Inanna well. We worked together regularly."

Oh. Fuck. I'm gonna have ta kill this man.

Annun pipes up this time. "So you know she's the one who stole Junco for two years and tortured her?"

Hando's eyes flash as we take a corner with speed and we all sway with the centripetal force. "I said worked, not work, alien. If I had known Inanna had Junco, I'd have stepped in. But we've not heard from her since the last time she brought HOUSE down here." He looks over at me now. "Which was the week after Junco was called home by the clone and never came back."

"Until last week, ya mean? She came back then, right?"

He smiles and slides his sunglasses down his face until his eyes are covered. "Do not piss me off, Beast. Because I don't need you to fix Junco's HOUSE AI. I have access to the Duality and I know you'll hand her over if it comes to that. So be nice to me and I'll let you tag along and watch."

Chapter Eleven

I think I might hate John Hando just a little bit more than Gideon. At least Gideon is one of us.

Sorta.

At least he's not human. And he's not a criminal. And I'm really starting to wonder if the Hando clan runs weapons when we pull up to the massive median level of the Sagitta Building, because there's about two dozen plasma cannons lifting up from subterranean concrete bunkers, and they are all targeting our vehicle.

Since John fucking Hando doesn't seem concerned about it, I can only assume they are there to target Annun and me.

"I strongly suggest," Hando says casually as the vehicle comes to a stop, "not to make any sudden moves, not to touch anything, and not to interact too closely with the AI in there. You got it?"

Annun answers for both of us with a wave of his hand. "Chill out, asshole. We're here to save the fucking kid, OK?"

I think I might like Annun a little more than I did an hour ago, but I shoot him the compulsory dirty look to placate our host.

HOUSE coughs as we exit and I lean down to whisper in her ear. "We're here now, darlin'. Just hold on." I have no idea if this being I'm holding like a child can die or not, but I can only assume it would be very bad luck to have something so connected to Junco expire on my watch.

The driver pulls away and we stand and wait as a well-dressed holographic man exits the front door and makes his way down a series of platformed steps. Hando presses an open palm in our direction, signaling to stay back, and then he approaches the quick-moving digitized being.

The AI does not look happy and I recall Junco's words from a few days ago about how male AI's are unstable. I've never actually thought about it before to be honest. We never had male AI's in The Band, but I always figured that's because Lucan was partial to the female versions.

HOUSE coughs again and this time I swear I can feel shit rattling around inside her. Hando waves us forward and I step up to the waiting AI, who does not greet me at all, but reaches out and tries to remove HOUSE from my arms.

I pull her back as his cold hands rub up against mine. It sends shivers up my spine and I realize instantly that my girl is not anything like this AI in front of me. "No. Yer not taking her."

He turns on his heel and begins walking up the steps and John Hando is following, beckoning us to come along. But my feet are plastered to the cement as I stare at what the AI shows us from behind.

It's another face.

A face so deformed it's hardly recognizable as female. Her bottom lip is mutilated and droops to one side and one eye is entirely missing. There is no hair to speak of, only a thin strip that gives the appearance of a hairline, but only if you see it from the proper angle. She catches my reaction and smiles and then speaks as they climb the steps in a lively manner—her knees bending in all the wrong places for someone who appears to be facing forward. I shiver again. "Keep up, Beast," is what I think she says, but I might be wrong because the sounds that emerge from her lips are so slurred and distorted it could be any number of things.

Annun looks at me with his eyebrows raised. "OK, looks like we're joining the freak show. Ready?" he asks me casually, as if he's the one in charge here and I might bolt or piss my pants at any minute. You gotta hand it to Annun. He's either a clueless dumbfuck or the most ballsy, well-informed son-of-a-bitch that ever walked this planet.

Our feet climb the steps in unison and when the AI and Hando have created a substantial distance between us, Annun leans in and whispers, "I read that the male did that to her face. He's a fucking psycho."

"Where'd ya read that?"

He shrugs. "I checked the sphere on the way over. What did you think I was doing? Sightseeing in the Underbelly?"

Annun's team points are stacking up today. I might have to promote him if we live through next week.

The AI stops at the front door and his fingers morph before my eyes, becoming nothing but a stream of electricity, and then connect to a receptor on the side of the building. The doors slide apart, but only wide enough to admit one man-sized person at a time. Hando goes first, then Annun, and I'm about to talk through when the AI abruptly turns and the female bends down to take a closer look at HOUSE with her good eye. I stop and let her scan the child, not sure if this is part of the process of gaining admittance or not. The body turns again and the male is apologizing. "She can step out of line at times, just know that she means no harm in this gesture. If she wasn't genuinely accepting of your presence here, you'd have been obliterated already."

I nod as I pass. Isn't that nice?

I've lost all sense of which duality is friendly. I go with neither and the door slides shut behind me.

The first thing that registers is that all my vision screen capabilities are cut off. The constant buzz that's been strumming though my head for more than two decades is suddenly gone. I look over at Annun and can tell he's experiencing the same thing, but he remains calm and begins to check out the interior decor.

The AI walks past me quickly, his holographic shoes producing a curt clicking sound on the polished granite floors for effect, and we all fall in line as we approach a bank of elevators that reside against the side of the building. "We've locked the building down since the invasion but we will allow you to see our engineer to determine if the HOUSE AI can be helped."

The AI stands there, waiting for me to answer, so I nod out a "We really appreciate you doing this," and then realize that Ashur must have given the relocation order since they think we've invaded.

"Just one thing," the AI continues. "If you had approached this building without that child, you would be riding a galactic wind as trillions of particles. Our cannons are SEAR-capable. We would not hesitate. We do not like you or what you're doing to our planet."

Annun winks and shoots his thumb and finger at the AI, then spurts out a good-natured, "Gotcha," before turning back to gape at the interior of the lobby.

The elevator opens and we all enter together. The biometrics protocol repeats, but this time John Hando does the honors and completes the biological inquisition with a drop of blood for an impromptu DNA scan.

He passes and I figure that's a good sign. And then the doors close and we are ascending the Sagitta Arrow.

Chapter Twelve

We stop long before we get to the top. I look over at Hando, but he ignores me. We exit into a long, slender, *dark*, corridor. It looks like the power went out and there's nothing lighting up the interior except emergency floodlights. The AI leads the way, and that grotesque face of the female stares at HOUSE as John Hando falls in line, then me, and Annun takes up the rear rifleman position out of habit. I can hear his uneven boot steps as he walks, and this comes off as a watch-your-back strategy most rear soldiers get when the fireteam is on the move.

Not that it matters, because if we get attacked in here, we're fucked. It's nothing but talons and razors because I have no porting power with the vision screen down. It pretty much runs all my gifts.

The AI stops at a door and waves John Hando forward. It surprises me how much access Hando actually has in this building. I don't know a whole lot about it other than it's exclusive, will kill you outright if you try to approach without clearance, and is run by the Duality—but I do know that no random Texican Mafia guy should be this well connected to it.

Which means John Hando's no random Texican Mafia guy.

The AI clears his throat and I direct my attention back to him to find them all waiting on me.

"What you will see is disturbing," the machine says without expression. "Just know that this was the choice of the Engineer."

John Hando doesn't wait for me to answer. He thumbs his genetics one more time and the wall slides up to reveal a large room, easily several stories high, filled with electronics, rows upon rows of processing power. My eyes scan it as quick as possible as we're ushered forward but it's not until I actually enter the room that I see what the AI was referring to.

It's a man.

Or probably not. Used to be a man might be a better description of the thing that sways in a tank of not-quite-clear fluid that looks, and smells, a lot like amniotic storage liquid.

HOUSE starts to choke, from the smell I think, and I have to use every mind trick I have not to bend over and retch.

"What the fuck is that smell?" Leave it to Annun to snap me back with an inappropriate comment.

"That smell is the decomposition of the Engineer," the AI replies. "Of course the preservatives are changed daily, but as you can imagine, it's not enough."

"What the fuck is it?" Annun asks. For once I'm glad he's here because protocol states you shut the fuck up in these types of situations, and I've been trained in protocol for so fucking long I'd never even think to start asking questions.

But Annun could give a shit.

"It's the baseline mind of the AI," Hando says. "Deb and Web are actually extensions of him. When he finally rots, we'll need to replace him. Why? How do you guys run your AI's?"

It takes me back for a moment and by the time I've recovered Annun is already answering.

"Nuclear power. Like the rest of the civilized fucking world."

Hando just shrugs, like he's clueless about how AI's are run and this is normal to him. I look behind me at footsteps. The AI has backed away and left us there. Probably uncomfortable coming face to face with its true form.

"Please tell me this child is not in a tank like that." I look over at Hando. "Or I think I will have to kill someone."

I expect Hando to get an attitude with me, deny it, and then threaten to kill me for threatening to kill him. But he doesn't. Which means HOUSE *is* in a tank like that.

"You've got to be fucking kidding me?"

"Tier, I did not make her, OK? I've been to her room once. Once. And that was when that Inanna bitch came and said we had to make adjustments if we wanted to save Junco."

I look down at HOUSE. "Is she dying? For real?"

Hando just shrugs and points to the far end of the room. "She's through that wall over there. Are you ready? Because it's a little more disturbing than this and she's looking pretty bad there in your arms, so—"

He lets his words drop.

"Let's go then, asshole. We gotta get in there now!" Annun is already halfway across the room when I give the nod.

We follow Annun.

Hando gives up some blood one more time and the wall slides up. If I thought the smell was bad in the first room, the pungent odor that affronts us now is like legions of bodies two weeks rotten on a summer battlefield.

If the view in front of me wasn't so—shocking—I might lean over and puke. But my eyes are focused on the true form of the girl wasting away in my arms.

Thousands upon thousands of amniotic tanks filled with little Junco clones.

"Holy fucking shit, Hando. What the fuck?" It dawns on me that maybe Gideon and Caleb do know about HOUSE, and maybe they knew that this was what she was, and maybe I *am* one fucked-up disturbed individual for keeping her around and treating her like a daughter.

"I knew," Hando says, quietly, "that this was wrong when I saw it before, but I had no way to know that she'd turn into this and regardless of what it looks like, I am not in charge here. Inanna is. She owns the building, she runs Deb and Web—I am not in charge of these abominations."

This statement refers not only to Junco clones floating in layer upon layer of tanks filed with cloudy liquid and which stack all the way to the ceiling, because honestly, if that's all that's going on here, I might be able to come to terms with it. But the clones are not even *whole* anymore. Limbs float in the fluid. Whole legs and arms, heads in some, dismembered from the main body.

They are in pieces.

"She cannot be fixed," I say to no one. "This cannot be fixed. Of all the things I've witnessed in my life, I could never imagine anyone being capable of doing this. Are they conscious?"

"The last time I was here—mind you, they looked a lot better—they were conscious then."

I walk up towards the nearest stack and peer into the cloudy liquid. It's almost opaque with… with what? Filth is the only word that comes to mind. Debris just doesn't cover it.

I walk along the aisle, peering into each one, searching for movement. Any sign that they are alive. It takes many rows of tanks before I find one that still has a recognizable face.

And her mouth is moving.

I watch her lips form the words. Over. And over.

And they say the same thing. Over. And over.
Kill me.

Kill me, they say. I look down at HOUSE and honest to God I want to kill something all right, but it's certainly not her.

"I have a better idea, Tier. If you're interested." John Hando's fingers grip my arm and pull me away from the begging child inside the tank. He pulls me all the way back into the Deb/Web room, seals the room back up, and then directs me to leave.

Annun is already outside, looking pale and spitting on the ground. The wall slides down and the smell evaporates with the filters that have since kicked on.

"There's no hope. She can't be saved."

"No, you're right. I'm going to order Web to cut the power and clean it all up. That is a mess. But there is hope for HOUSE, Tier. The Sagitta is a lot of things, but an office building is not one of them. It's an advanced weapons system, it's a sentient AI, and it's a transmitter."

I barely know what he's talking about, the image of Junco in those tanks is burned into me. "That's why they cloned her?"

Hando seems to want to get past this topic quickly, so he just nods. "Partially, I'd assume. I have no idea who's been up here or how often. If they changed them out or whatever. I could ask Web if you really want to—"

"No," I say. "No, I don't want to know."

"Me either, man. Me either. I don't want to know."

"But why? Why do this?" I look over at him and shake my head. "What did they get from it?"

"That's what I'm trying to explain. When Inanna came that time she told me if the tanks should ever fail I was to beam the mind up through the transmitter."

I just stare at him.

He points up. "The transmitter. In the top of the Arrow. She said it would shoot the core AI out into space. Why that's a good idea, I don't know but that's—"

"Wait!" Annun is back in action and we both turn. "Junco's out there, scattered into particles, right? If we shoot HOUSE up there, maybe she'll go back inside Junco? Or maybe she'll pull her back together and Juncs will come back?"

We all look at each other like a bunch of idiots. I've heard dumber things in my time, that's for sure. I've tried dumber things, actually. "OK, let's try that. Can we try it now?"

Hando's already on the move and Annun and I follow, our steps much quicker going back through the dark narrow hallway than they were coming down it.

This time we take the elevator down to the bottom floor, then catch another one that will take us up to the top of the Arrow.

HOUSE coughs in my arms and I lean heavily on the stainless steel wall and let out a sigh. This is not going at all how I planned. I'm not sure what I thought would be here at the Sagitta, but it wasn't what I found. And if ya would've told me a few hours ago that HOUSE would be dead by evening, I probably would've ripped yer face off.

But this is reality. She is dying. I'm not taking her back to Sargassum. Her beach days are over. There will be no more flipflops, no more peanut butter and jelly sandwiches, and no more half-hearted parenting from me.

It's not fair.

It's not fucking fair that I have to give everything up just as I start to get attached to it. And maybe it's not the best time to be lamenting on things like this, but shit.

The elevator stops and the doors slide open. Annun leads the way out and we follow. It's a very small room made out of glass that opens up to the night sky so that all you see are stars. I can only imagine the delight Junco got from this view. I stop for a moment to appreciate it, then look around me.

My vision screen is still offline, but if it wasn't, I'd bet my life that these windows were made of fused quartz. The floors are covered with a deep red carpet and a spiral staircase winds around the elevator housing and leads up to a platform that is the literal top to the Sagitta.

"Take her up there, I'll go get things ready and then come back."

I nod and then address Annun. "Go with him." He makes to balk about it, but then studies my face, takes a long look at HOUSE in my arms, and changes his mind.

They both get back in the elevator and then we are alone.

"I got ya, HOUSE. Yer gonna be OK, girl. Ya got it?"
She moans.

I climb the steps and walk out onto the platform. The windows are so clear it feels like you're standing on a cloud. I lie down in the middle of the floor and put the little girl on my chest. She coughs and this time a little bit of blood comes out of her mouth.

"Yer gonna go see Junco now, HOUSE, but I'm gonna tell ya a story before ya go, OK? Because Gideon fucked it all up when he told it to her and if she's decided to leave us for good, well, I think she deserves to know the truth about how it ends."

I wait for an acknowledgment, but get silence instead.
So I start on my own.

"When everything was evil, in the time before now, there was a God's princess. She took the shape of a beautiful swan and she soared in the sky every night, looking for her friends. She knew them all, they were like brothers and sisters to her. But there was a boundary to her world, a great river of stars that cut the galaxy in half. She could often be found sitting next to the river desperately trying to see across it—because she knew there was another bird over there. An eagle. Jupiter's eagle. She'd seen him many times, even called out to him once, but he never responded. Maybe he couldn't hear her, or maybe he was ignoring her, it didn't matter. She wanted to talk to him but it was impossible to get his attention and it was impossible to cross the river of stars.

"Then one day the God's swan princess was soaring towards the river when she spied a little fox. The swan knew the fox, she was the daughter of a very famous fox, and a cunning little animal who was known for her tricks and antics in the swan princess' realm. So the swan approached the little fox and made a proposition. If the little fox would devise a way to cross the river of stars, she would bestow a gift on her."

"What was the gift?" HOUSE's little voice croaks.

The ache in my heart is so strong I almost can't continue. I squeeze her gently and tuck down the hurt. "Darlin', the swan promised the little fox that if she helped her cross the river she'd make sure that Jupiter's arrow would never find her as its target."

"But Jupiter's arrow always finds its mark," HOUSE mumbles.

She's so smart. I smile because she's so smart. It is so appropriate that Junco's HOUSE knows the myths of the sky. "I know, darlin', that's why the gift was so special. It set up a paradox, just like her father, the Teumessian fox, had with Laelaps the dog."

Silence this time.

"The God's swan princess caused a big rift in the night sky with this promise. And all the gods and goddesses were afire with anger and unease. They wanted her to take the gift back, but the swan princess tilted her chin high and refused. She wanted to cross the river of stars and meet Jupiter's eagle."

"And," HOUSE adds softly, "she wanted to keep her little fox alive too, right?"

"That's exactly right. She liked the little fox, no—she loved the little fox. And the little fox came up with a trick to help her cross the river. She asked all the birds of the sky to come help make a bridge across the galaxy, but none of the important birds would disobey the other gods and goddesses. Only the trouble-making magpies agreed to the little fox's request. So on the third day of the ninth month, the magpies flew to the river of stars and spread their wings so the God's swan princess could cross the river on the magpie bridge."

"What happened to the fox?" she asks, barely a whisper.

"Darlin', this is the best part so make sure that when you see Junco up there in the sky ya tell her, OK?"

Silence.

"When Jupiter's eagle saw the God's swan princess he fell instantly in love with her and when she told him of the trouble she caused just to get to him, the eagle promised to protect the little fox from Jupiter's arrow forever."

I wait for my little fox to respond but her breath is shallow and she's going very pale.

The elevator doors open then and Annun and Hando come out. "Tier?" Annun calls.

"Up here."

I listen to his boots climb the stairs and when he gets to the top he's out of breath and red-faced. "You've got about thirty seconds, then the transmission will start."

I nod and he goes back down, leaving us alone.

"That's not the end, Little Fox. Yer gonna miss the end if ya leave me now."

"How's it end, Tier?" Her words do not even qualify as a whisper but I hear them and force myself to continue.

"It ends with the eagle giving up everything to spend eternity with the God's swan princess. Not for one night a year, darlin'. *Forever.*"

My heart beats in my chest like it's gonna explode as I wait for her reply, but HOUSE is gone. I feel the coldness sweep through and the life leave her body as her heart stops pumping.

I look up to the infinite depths of space and hope as the transmission manifests as a pure white light.

I let go of the girl and shield my eyes, and when the light is gone—so is my Little Fox.

Chapter Thirteen

I get up and look down at my warrior and John Hando. "Dude, you are so fucking dead," Annun states matter-of-factly. "I sure hope HOUSE went up in the sky, because man, Junco is gonna be one pissed-off little psycho when she gets back and finds out you dissipated her HOUSE!"

I think I love Annun. I think he's Braun and Isten all twisted together in one obnoxious asshole and I think I love Annun because he believes in me. In us. In himself. In Junco. He's so Goddamned simple and honest.

My wings unfurl and I jump down to the ground. Hando just raises his eyebrows at me and shakes his head. "I think it worked, man. I really do. She disappeared, and I think that's a good sign."

I'm still thinking about this when the elevator doors open and the Web AI exits. "Mr. Hando, there are avian warriors outside demanding to see the Captain and this"— he looks Annun up and down with an obvious disdain— "warrior. They have urgent messages for them."

Hand looks at me. "You done here? Or you want me to go grab the message and bring it to you?"

I look up at the top of the Sagitta building one more time. It's not called the Arrow for nothing. It *is* the arrow. Jupiter's arrow, the constellation in the sky that sits in front of Aquila the eagle, is called Sagitta.

"No, I'm ready. We did all we could. Caleb says Junco is coming home, and I trust him. He would not lie to me. We did what we could."

We all enter the elevator together and stand in silence as we descend back to earth. Downstairs I can see my warriors even though I can't hear them. The building is soundproof, but there's no denying that what's going on outside is almost out-and-out war.

"Can you give me tech access so I can tell them to stand down?" I address Web, not Hando this time.

The AI stares at me for a second, then nods. "Of course, Captain."

My vision screen comes to life and I have several hundred waiting messages. I clear them all and order a ceasefire.

Most of the battle comes to a halt, and then I notice Web's vacant stare and figure he's called off his rockets or whatever the hell he has out there.

The doors slide open and we all exit together.

Tessen is running up to Annun talking wildly while Pike and Merkar shove her aside and try to take over. I ignore them and look to Arel instead.

"Anything change?"

He nods. "Yeah, there's some movement in the Seventh, but it's not all that spectacular."

"I'm gonna go back to Peak City and wait it out, OK? If you guys—"

"Tier!" Annun is running up to me now. "Wait! They found her!"

The wave of nausea that rumbles through my stomach makes me swallow hard. "They found who, Annun?"

"The baby," he whispers.

I look around to see if anyone else heard. Arel has already moved on but John Hando is still next to me so I play it down. "You have standing orders, Annun. Carry them out." I turn to walk away and put an end to this conversation.

"Tier!" This time it's Tessen. I turn just in time to see Merkar and Pike yank her back by the arms, but she elbows Pike in the chin and he lets go just as she knocks Merkar down with a well-placed foot sweep and runs over to me. "I'm not on board with this, do you understand? I am not on board!"

"I don't care, Tessen. I gave the order. All you have to do is carry it out. If you refuse, then get the fuck off my team." I stare at her and wait for her defiance but she stands down, not willing to lose her position I suppose. But she does find her voice.

"I want to hear you issue that order again then, Captain. So when Junco gets back I can tell her I heard those words come straight out of your mouth."

I let out a long tired breath. "Do you know what that thing is, Tessen?"

She just shrugs and begins to talk softly. "It doesn't matter what it is. Things can be killed but they can never be unkilled. If you do this, Tier, you'll regret it. And let's face it, we've all collected up enough regrets for one lifetime, don't you think?"

I look over her shoulder at Pike and Merk and sigh. "Drug it into unconsciousness and contain it." I stare at her eyes and watch them reflect the red in my own. "If you let that thing wake up and get out, Tessen, I'll—"

But she's already running back to her team.

"What the hell was that all about?"

"Exactly what it sounded like, Hando."

I wait for the judgment I deserve but he stays silent for a few moments. "Hey," he finally says with some sympathy. "You got a place to stay? You want to come meet my family?"

"What?"

He shrugs and pulls out a com, swipes his fingers a few times as he stares down at it. "I have a nice family, Tier. You'll love them. And they love Junco to death. Let's wait it out at my house." He ushers me over to his vehicle and pushes me into the back. He climbs in next to me and puts his com away. "They'll come back, I think."

"Maybe," I say. "Or maybe we'll just all be dead in a few days."

"Yeah," Hando says without malice or anger. "You probably have other people you'd like to hang out with then. You got your own family and stuff? You don't have to come home with me. I get it."

Who do I have?

Lucan and Rikan are with Amelia, Sera is who knows where, Ashur has Selia, Annun and the fledgling team are working, Ryse wants to kick my ass over Esta, and Arel is way too busy to hang out. Braun would've been my first choice, but he's dead.

I look out the window, search for the stars, and then point up. "They're up there, John. They're both up there."

They are the only two people I care about right now. They are all I have left.

And I *would* sell my soul, I would give up my promised eternal salvation, if I could just get one more chance to make it right for them.

End of Book Shit

Tier. Sigh. Enough said. :)

ABOUT THE AUTHOR

JA Huss is the New York Times Bestselling author of 321 and has been on the USA Today Bestseller's list 21 times in the past four years. She writes characters with heart, plots with twists, and perfect endings.

Her books have sold millions of copies all over the world, the audio version of her semi-autobiographical book, Eighteen, was nominated for a Voice Arts Award and an Audie Award in 2016 and 2017 respectively, her audiobook, Mr. Perfect, was nominated for a Voice Arts Award in 2017, and her audiobook, Taking Turns, was nominated for an Audie Award in 2018. Five of her book were optioned for a TV series by MGM television in 2018.

She lives on a ranch in Central Colorado with her family.